Karl Francis was born in Bedwas, Caerphilly. He studied the Slade School of Fine Art, and the Hornsey Art and Film School. After working as a teacher, he began making documentaries in the early 1970s and started making films in 1972.

Since then he has worked independently, until joining the BBC Wales drama department as an executive producer in 1994. In January 1996 he was appointed Head of Drama, BBC Wales.

His film credits include *Above us the Earth* (1977); *Giro City* (1984) which starred Glenda Jackson and Jon Finch; *The Happy Alcoholic*, which was voted outstanding film of the year at the London Film Festival; *Boy Soldier* (1986), which won prizes at Mannheim, Chicago and Sorrento; *Angry Earth* (1988); *Murder in Oaklands* (1991) and *Judas and the Gimp* (1993).

For BBC Wales he has made *Ms Rhymney Valley (1985)*; *1996* (1989); *Morphine and Dolly Mixtures* (1990); *Rebecca's Daughters* (1991) and *Civvies* (1992).

STREETLIFE

BY

KARL FRANCIS

An Original Screenplay

PARTHIAN BOOKS

First published 1996 by Parthian Books
41 Skelmuir Road, Cardiff CF2 2PR

Published with financial support from the
Arts Council of Wales

© Karl Francis 1995
All rights reserved

ISBN 0 952 1558 4 2

Printed and bound in the United Kingdom
Typeset in New Sabon by JW.

British Library Cataloguing in Publication Data.
A cataloguing record for this book is available from
the British Library.

This book is sold subject to the condition that it shall
not, by way of trade or otherwise, be circulated
without the publisher's prior consent in any form of
binding or cover other than that in which it is
published and without a similar condition including
the condition being imposed on the subsequent
purchaser.

Contents

Streetlife	7
Cast	74
Notes on a Film	77
Diary	81

OPENING SEQUENCE: INT. IRONING ROOM - TOILETS.

JANICE, LYNWEN, JO, SHARON, GAIL, DONALD.

SHARON *and* ANNIE *make up in the mirror.*
JANICE: Eh, did you hear about the woman who goes to the doctor as she's got problems down below – he says, you've got trouble with your avaries – don't you mean ovaries she said, no, you've had a cock or two up there.
GIRLS *laugh.*
Another woman being examined by her doctor, legs all strapped up, he says, haven't you got a big fanny, haven't you got a big fanny. She says, alright, no need to say it twice. He says, I didn't.
GIRLS *laugh.*
GAIL *and* LYNWEN *exit.*
JANICE: A man buys a Skoda, he goes back to complain, saying it'll only go up to 80 on a hill. That's not bad he's told, it is he replied, I live at 92.
JO *knocks on the toilet door.*
DONALD: (*From inside loo.*) Eh, it's me.
ANDREA *comes out of other loo.*
JO: I'm worried about you.
DONALD: Come on girls, we'll be late.
They exit.

Scene 1: EXT IRONING ROOM STREET.

DONALD: She said, you can't be Phyllis Morgan's son, you've gone fat and bald.

GAIL: There's a woman out there, married for 26yrs., her husband beat her every weekend, he died last month, she's missing him like hell.

ANDREA: Our Jo, she's got a new boyfriend.

What's his name?

JO: Kevin, I told you.

ANDREA: On his birth certificate?

JO: Kevin Price.

ANDREA: He's famous he is, first test tube baby.

JO: I'm off

JO *looks up to the sky on a beautiful day. Anxiety on her face, in the background* DONALD *and* JANICE *unload the van.*

JANICE: Lovely day.

JO: I been praying for rain.

JANICE: The garden?

JO: No, the bloody council.

GAIL *walks by.*

GAIL: The trick is to get as many points as you can, make sure all the windows are open so it's freezing. Borrow my kids if it helps.

JO: Wish me luck.

JO *licks her finger and holds it up to feel the way of the wind.*

ANDREA: Our Jo's going to college.

SHARON: She'll be all airs and graces then.

GAIL: Oprah says men dally with love for sex and women dally with sex for love.

Scene 2: EXT FRONT DOOR.
KEVIN *gets into the van.* TRISH, *his young wife is tearful, exhausted; stares confused, angry yet accepting at her husband.*
TRISHA: Who is she? Who's the tart?
   (*To her son.*) Stay here, I'm talking to your father.
KEVIN *is silent. His* SON *enters the frame.*
TRISHA: Well if I was you I'd take a polaroid, just don't get involved.
KEVIN: I am involved.
He's an attractive working class thinker type. Depardieu in a suit. His personality is bland, subtle. He seems safe, is social, good looking, not sophisticated. A charming wide boy. He drives off.

Scene 3: EXT. TERRY'S HOUSE
JO *walks along prominently carrying Boots bag, containing pregnancy test.*
JO *walks up street.*
SANDIE: Hiya Jo
JO: Hiya Sandie.
JO *enters house.*

Scene 4: EXT JO'S DAD'S HOUSE.
KEVIN'S *van stands idly outside. The house is in an estate of rented council houses and is in a poor state of repair.*
KEVIN *approaches the house.*
JO: Hiya (*Kiss.*) Dad, this is Kev.
TERRY: Leave me out of it. I don't want to know.
TERRY *leaves.*
KEV: What time's the engineer coming?

JO: Any minute.
KEV: Plenty of time.
JO: Kev!
KEV *chases* JO *inside, pulling his trousers down as he goes. They make love in the hall.*

Scene 5: EXT. TERRY'S HOUSE.
THE ENGINEER CYCLES TO AND APPROACHES TERRY'S HOUSE.
ENGINEER *walks up path.*
JO: (*From hallway.*) It's him. He's coming.
  Do you know what you're doing?
KEVIN *rushes upstairs to fix the 'leak'.*
JO *answers the door to the engineer.*
JO: (JO *looks up to blue sky.*) It's not raining is it?
ENGINEER: (*puzzled.*) Don't think so.

Scene 6: INT. TERRY'S HOUSE.
The ENGINEER *has a good look round.* KEVIN *crouches in the loft. The water pours in.*
JO: I mean, when it rains it's really bad. My daughter's got a permanent cold.
(*Pointing to damp in bedroom.*) Look at that, it never dries out, sweats, and it's not even raining.
ENGINEER: Can I look in the loft?
JO (*Fetches the* ENGINEER *a chair.*): Can you hold this please?
Inside the loft KEVIN *rushes to brace himself against the loft door. Below the* ENGINEER, *stands on a chair. He fails to shift it.*
ENGINEER: Got a step ladder?
JO: Sorry.
ENGINEER: Right, I'll just have to pop outside to have a look

The ENGINEER *and* JO *go outside. The* ENGINEER *looks up at roof.*
KEV *is in loft shifting slates.*
The women are all waiting at the garden wall.
ANDREA: She's not having my bed again, I had to sleep on the floor.
LYNWEN: She can't come and live with me. I'm not having it.
ENGINEER: (*To* JO, *about the roof.*) Can't your husband sort it out?
LYNWEN: My ex you mean. I wouldn't ask him. If it rained soup he'd go out with a fork.
GAIL: Three million on the dole and you pick on her.
ENGINEER: Now, let's get this straight . . . she lives here with her daughter . . .
LYNWEN: (*Interrupts.*) She lives here with my ex and her daughter Lily. She lives with me, that's Andrea, and I've got osteoporosis, I'll be in a wheelchair in 3 yrs.
ANDREA: And my father's an alcoholic. . .
ABBIE: You have to find her a house.
GAIL: It's like Custer's last stand and we're the Indians.
   Come on love, on yer bike.
The ENGINEER *laughs. He leaves.*
KEVIN *is still in the loft. He hears the door shut and then plugs up the tank. Hands return the slates to their proper place. The water stops dripping.*
JO: Kev! Kev!
   He'll do anything for a shag!
KEVIN *opens the trap door to the loft. He enters the garden.*
KEVIN'S *arm is held proudly by* JO.
It's KEVIN'S *turn to feel like General Custer as all the girls stare at him.*

ABBIE: I know you, you live down by me.
KEVIN: See you then.
JO *lets him go, smiling sweetly.* KEVIN *shuffles off. Laughter follows him.*
JO: I'm lucky see, he's there for me.
LYNWEN: What about his wife ?
JO: She's holding him back.
GAIL: I think she's in love.
JO: I am. People are like Christmas presents – me to you, you to me. It's nice.
LYNWEN: There are the bad times though, Jo.
JO: But you see them through, don't you.

Scene 7:   INT. TERRY'S HOUSE.
JO *does the urine sample and the blue litmus indicates she is pregnant.*

Scene 8: EXT. APPROACHING COLLEGE.
JO & LILY *travelling on top of double decker bus. We see the College.*
JO: Look Lily, there's the college.

Scene 9: EXT. TECHNICAL COLLEGE.
JO *pushes* LILY *through crowds of students, she meets up with* ANDREA.

Scene 10: INT. CAFETERIA COLLEGE.
Faces look steamy. Hot water on coffee. JO *goes to counter. Puts Cappuccino down and an orange juice.* JO *watches the cashier's till. The prices rush up. Establish* JO'S *sense of poverty. Not deserving.*

Streetlife

CASHIER: 10p for hot water.
JO (*Whispers.*): . . . the coffee was cold. . .
Pause. JO *calls her bluff.*
CASHIER: Sorry, 10p for hot water.
JO *looks over* ANDREA *is there with a parcel sitting by* LILY. JO *walks across.*
ANDREA *is reading* JO'S *notes conscientiously.*
ANDREA: You look great.

You gotta pay Jo, that's bloody wrong that is.

JO: Ssh, they pay some, I pay the rest.
ANDREA: Here you are -
ANDREA *gives* JO *the parcel. She opens it up; it's a briefcase.* JO *smiles.*
JO: What is it? Where'd you get this?

Thanks Andy.

ANDREA: This bloke I've got – Marzi – is useless in bed.
(ANDREA *shows photo of* MARZI *and* ANDREA.)

The first time we had sex was with my leg, (ANDREA *mimics premature ejaculation.*) and it was over in a minute. I've got him a lot better mind.

Well, tell me . . . why do men think when you go ooh, aah, it's real and wonderful? I suppose they have to.

How's it with Kevin?

JO: Fantastic...
ANDREA: I'll have him then.

(*Pause.*) This won't change you, will it Jo?

JO: Don't be stupid.
JO *leaves.*

Bye bye Lily.

Scene 11: INT. COLLEGE – LECTURE ROOM.
JO *enters lecture room during lecture.*
LECTURER: So, Wittgenstein the philosopher, risked having a homosexual love affair here in Pontypridd, as did Merton, the American monk, who risked having an illegitimate child. They were men of passion. So how does Merton put it in his book – To hope, he says, is to risk frustration. Do not be one of those who, rather than risk failure, never attempt anything. What's he saying? You've got to risk being yourself.

Scene 12: EXT. ON RIVER. EVENING.
JO *watches* LILY *playing very happily with the ducks. She picks* LILY *up and swings her around.*
JO *with flowers in big close up.* JO *breathes in the petals tickling her first.*
JO: Daffodil.
LILY: Fi . . . affo . . .
JO: Dil.
JO *looks up at the stars. Happiness itself.*
JO: Star. You mother's a star, Lily.

Scene 13: COUNCIL HOUSE. INT/EXT. GAIL *is mutton dressed up as lamb, worn out beauty in her thirties. They make their way upstairs to* JO'S *new home.*
GAIL: I've seen bloody worse than this.
They reach door. JO *puts* LILY *down.*
GAIL: Give her to me. Come to Aunty Gail. Your mother's excited.
The house is a mess. It badly needs painting and repairing. Windows are barricaded. JO *comes into the room. Her new home.*

JO: What d'you think? Bit of paint?
GAIL: And the rest. Don't worry, the council'll clean it up.
GAIL *goes to barricaded window.*
   And you've got a garden.
   Come on, we haven't got all day.

Scene 14:   GAIL'S FLAT. EXT/INT.
The flat is poor but smart. Someone's struggling for a West Coast look. JO, LILY *and* GAIL *approach..* LILY *is left outside with* GAIL'S *kids.*
GAIL: (*To* KIDS *outside.*) Mammy's going in.
   You play with Lily.
The PHOTOGRAPHER *gets off the bus and approaches.*
GAIL: It's the photographer, he's early.
JO AND GAIL RUSH INTO THE HOUSE.
GAIL: Put these on, quick.
The PHOTOGRAPHER *comes into the house. Just a Polaroid camera. Looks at his watch.*
PHOTOGRAPHER: Sorry 'bout this. You the girl?
ANNIE: No, you had me last week, remember?
JO: Hiya. Where's the lights?
PHOTOGRAPHER: No lights. Just you love. Upstairs OK, follow me.
GAIL: He knows the way. Don't let him photo your face, alright?
JO *and* PHOTOGRAPHER *go upstairs.*
PHOTOGRAPHER: Come on love, get them off.

Scene 15:   GAIL'S HOUSE. EXT.
A CREDITOR *approaches in van via back lane.*
The three men knock the door. They want to collect some of the furniture.

Streetlife

GAIL: What do you want?
CREDITOR:: We've come for your furniture, Gail.
GAIL: What d'you mean now, you come for my furniture?
CREDITOR: We're from the bailiff's office. We've gotta have your bed.
GAIL: You can have the bed tomorrow, you can take the sofa now.

The men remove the sofa.

Scene 16: UPSTAIRS BEDROOM. INT.
JO *is looking out the window. The* PHOTOGRAPHER *photographs her from behind.*
JO: Hey, listen, you sure you don't copy those do you?
PHOTOGRAPHER: No, I promise. That's it, lean forward a bit, stick your bum in the air, that's better.
JO: You're a bloody pervert, you are.
PHOTOGRAPHER: Takes all sorts, love.
Outside the window, ANDREA *comes up the path.*
JO: Damn. It's my sister.

The PHOTOGRAPHER *pops out. We get a glimpse of* JO'S *backside. Tenners exchange hands.*
JO *darts into the bathroom.*
JO: I'm having a pee, Gail! (*Shouts.*)
   (*To* PHOTOGRAPHER.) Can I have the money, now, quickly? Stay in here.

Scene 17: INT. DOWNSTAIRS.
ANDREA *comes down* GAIL'S *garden path as* BAILIFFS *leave with sofa.*

ANDREA *breezes through the house.*
ANDREA: Hiya, is Jo here?
GAIL: Yeah, she's upstairs in the toilet.
ANDREA: OK if I go up?
GAIL: Go on.
ANDREA: Lend us a tenner Gail?
GAIL: Get lost Andrea.
ANDREA GOES UPSTAIRS.
ANDREA: Hey Jo, lend us a tenner. I'm going shopping.
JO: How d'you know I was here?
JO SHOVES A TENNER UNDER THE DOOR.
ANDREA: Ta love, see you Jo.
ANDREA *goes downstairs into the Kitchen. The* BAILIFFS *are leaving with the sofa.*
ANDREA: Gail, what's happening?
GAIL: Bastard bailiffs.

Scene 18: INT. BEDROOM.
JO *rejoins the* PHOTOGRAPHER *in the bedroom, almost knocking him ove. He's been listening at the door.*
JO: She's gone.
PHOTOGRAPHER: Thanks, fine. OK?
    I'd lose some weight, if I were you.
This makes JO *think, she stares in the mirror and smiles to herself.*

Scene 19: INTERIOR. FAMILY PLANNING OFFICE.
JO *is being examined by the* FPA DOCTOR.
DOCTOR: Fifteen weeks seems about right I think.
JO: Fifteen weeks!

Streetlife

DOCTOR: You're very small, it doesn't show. Don't be surprised if you're early. Are you sure you want the baby?
JO: I dunno.
DOCTOR: Look Jo, I'd tell him if I were you.
    The sooner the better. OK?

Scene 20:   OLD COAL MINE. EXT.
JO *pushes the pram with* LILY *in it and carries the two black bags along the trail where the old colliery used to be. The wheels of the pram crush over dead needles. She joins her mother,* LYNWEN, *who looks around the abandoned broken colliery, remembering.*
JO: Hullo Mam. I thought I'd find you here.
LYNWEN: Hi babe, come to your nanny then.
    (*To* LILY.) Look what they've done to the old pit – it's getting old now, they used to make coal here.
    See over there, where the mines used to be.
She lifts LILY *up*.
    What's the matter Jo?
JO: I'm pregnant Mam . . .
LYNWEN: Oh Jo -
JO: I love him . . . I'm happy Mam . . . the first time in years . . .
    You don't like him do you?
LYNWEN: He's a married man . . . I don't trust him that's all.
    You should have worked it out with Mark. How far gone is it?
JO: 10 weeks. What shall I do Mum?
LYNWEN: I'll help you all I can. (*Pause.*) If I was you I'd get rid of it . . .
She hugs JO.

Scene 21: IRONING ROOM. INT.
The ironing room is a modern sweat shop in a rented building. A group of eight women are talking and ironing piles of clothes in black bags standing around. JO *enters and picks up a black bag of ironing and starts to iron. She listens to the radio and watches* LILY *enjoy herself with two other children. Heavy rock music is on the radio, interrupted by news, including the 10th anniversary of the Miners' Strike and the following:*
RADIO INSERT
'Police are investigating the death of a 6 year old girl at her home in Swansea. DCI Keith Williams said the girl's mother had found her body lying in her own bed. Neighbours said that the little girl, whose name was Claire, was a picture of health. The girl's mother is helping the police.'
Then cut to ROCK MUSIC.

SHARON: What I do when I do the business is keep everything separate – clothes, bedroom – so when I put on my evening clothes I don't want to be reminded of some creep whose dick I was sucking.

ANNIE: I'm going out with this creep, he's 50 and still hasn't got a clue how to kiss a woman.

(*On to* LYNWEN & JANICE.)

JANICE: You tell me then, how do I tell people my son is a heroin addict? I can't afford to go under. (*Pause.*)
They leave school . . . no jobs . . .

LYNWEN: I don't see what they get out of it. In a stupor all the time, and they're stealing. (*Pause, to iron.*)

JANICE: You always think it's someone else's children.

LYNWEN: And there's the social stigma. You can't say to the butcher when he asks how you feel 'OK, but my daughter's a

heroin addict.'
ANDREA: Mam!
JANICE: The police must be thick. I told them Acker was a dealer six months ago.
LYNWEN: Ssh . . .
The look over to GAIL, *who's* ACKER'S *wife.*
JANICE: At least I can throw the money at him.
JO: What do you mean, throw the money at him?
JANICE: So, what you think they do with the money? You can't be that naive, Jo.
LYNWEN *picks up* LILY *and hands her to* JO.
JO: Daddy won't be long.
GAIL: Try this on. (GAIL *passes* JO *a blouse.*)
JO: Ta. It's lovely. (GAIL *laughs.*)
GAIL: Kiss, kiss Lily.
(ANNIE *walks through, talking to* SHARON.)
ANNIE: I'm a flirt, I'm terrible. But I told Tony, if you weren't any good at sex I wouldn't want to know.
JANICE: Don't talk to me about men. Money it is. All the arguments in our house are about money.
Seen these?
They look at photos of caravan.
My caravan, in Ogmore, anytime you want to use it . . .
JO *laughs working hard. She drops bags at* DONALD'S *feet. The boss is there.*
JO: Pay him the rate. Geraint. (*To* DONALD.) Stand up for yourself.
MARK *walks in.* JO *kisses* MARK.
Hey, Mark . . . What d'you think of this?
He picks up LILY. MARK *is* JO'S *ex.*

MARK: Nice one. Hi Lily.
   How's my girl then? Come to your Dad, then.
LILY *is very comfortable with him.* MARK *rubs noses with her.*
MARK *grabs shirt off ironing board.*
   That's my shirt by there.
   Eh Jo, if you're not back by 9 o'clock I'll leave her with
   Lynwen, OK?
JO: Thanks.
MARK *acknowledges* LYNWEN *and leaves with* LILY.
JANICE: He's a nice boy.
LYNWEN: They were courting in school. Mark is too nice for our
   Jo. She walks all over him.
JO *smiles. She is now dressed in a smart suit.*
JO: Aye . . . 'til I caught him with that slag from Splott . . . what I
   should have done was rip his head off his cowing shoulders . .
   . I was glad to see the back of him.
JO *takes a black bag and piles it on another.*
JO: I'd rather go with a lesbian than go with him again.
   What do you think? (JO *looks beautiful.*)
   'We are family, I got all my sisters with me . . .'
The other girls join in.

Scene 22: EXT. COUNTRYSIDE.
In a pretty and lyrical scene, JO *and* KEVIN *dissolve into the hillside. The sunlight is warm, the colours soft.*
KEVIN *starts to kiss her and fumbles at her clothes.* JO *is very happy.*
JO: You'll love it Kev, all it needs is a coat of paint.
KEVIN *is touching her stomach and continues to fondle* JO.
JO: . . . And I've enrolled at the Tech . . . I got to write this essay

Streetlife

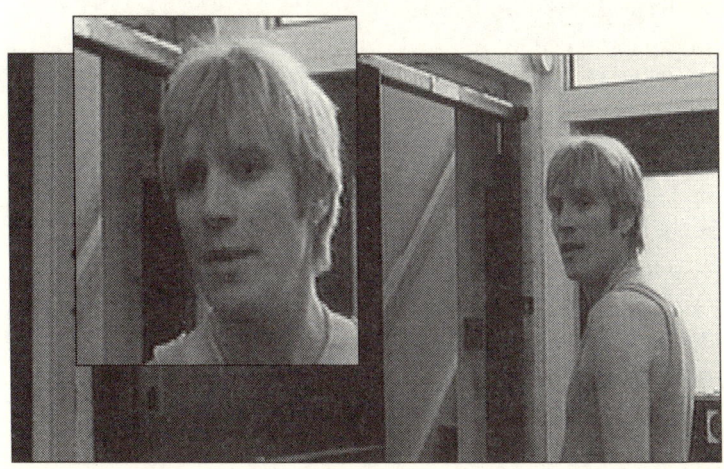

about psychology and the environment.
KEVIN: Fucking hell. You are big. You're not pregnant are you?
JO: Kevin! No I'm not. What if I was?
KEVIN (*Pulls a face.*)
   But you're not, are you ?
JO: . . . I asked Lily's Dad to help out with her.
KEVIN: Why'd you do that?
   If you want help, I'll pay for it. I don't see why he should be in the house all the time.
JO: He's Lily's father.
KEVIN: OK. Come here.
He kisses her.
JO: Please.
KEVIN: Please. We'll get married, OK.
JO: Yeah, when you get divorced and when you're serious, yeah, course I will Kevin.
KEVIN: Great.
JO: Kev.
KEVIN *kisses her.*
JO: Oh, Kev. I love you Kev. . . .
KEVIN: I love you Jo.
JO *kisses him passionately, overwhelmingly.*

Scene 23: GARAGE INT.
ANDREA *is being felt up by a middle aged man,* EDDIE. ANDREA *is 'eating' a bag of chips, not ostentatiously, but enough to demonstrate her mind is on other things.* EDDIE *fumbles at her thighs.*
ANDREA: Chip Ed? I eat chips for Wales.
   Tits first.

EDDIE: Sorry.
EDDIE dissolves into a flood of tears and what began as a rough sexual scene dissolves into tenderness.
ANDREA: She's not coming back, is she Ed?
EDDIE: She won't.
Despite the tenderness, ANDREA'S eyes wander to EDDIE'S wrist and an expensive Rolex.
ANDREA: Hey, that's enough. Where'd you get that from? I'll have that.

Scene 24: STREET. EXT.
ANDREA comes out of garage. On her wrist, the Rolex. JO and KEVIN kiss passionately. JO spots ANDREA.
JO: Andrea?
JO chases ANDREA upstairs into drug house.
JO & ANDREA arrive in room where the junkies are hanging out.
ACKER: What d'you want?
JO: (*Notices Rolex.*) Where'd you get that?
ANDREA: Go home Jo. Get out.
ACKER: (*To* ANDREA.) Bag?
JO leaves.

Scene 25: INT. GARAGE. NIGHT.
A tired out scene. ANDREA joins the junkies hanging out. MARZI injects himself with heroin. ANDREA smokes heroin.
Chasing the Dragon: Milk bottle tops, plastic Coke bottles with the bottoms sliced off – heroin paraphernalia. ANDREA is not injecting. MARZI notices this.
MARZI: The last time . . . right?
ACKER: Yeah Marzi, the last time.

Scene 26: EXT. LYNWEN'S HOUSE. DAY.
JO *walks* LILY *along garden wall to* LYNWEN.

LYNWEN: I had my friends around the room
              All I could feel was gloom and doom
              Then the 10 was on the spoon
              My life was now heroin bound

              At 17, things – they got us down
              I fought the state, I took the brown
              No work, no hope, I'd lie awake
              Dreaming and planning the great escape

JO *looks at poem,* LYNWEN *hides it behind her back as* ANDREA *approaches.*
JO: You alright?
ANDREA: No, Marzi wants to marry me, that's all. I want to stop, I can't.
ANDREA *rushes into house,* JO *follows her.*

Scene 27:   ADDICT STREET. EXT.
Camera tracks along. Sisters music. ANDREA *and* JO *walking. Sisters. Annie Lennox.* ANDREA *is withdrawing, cold turkeying it.*
ANDREA: It's cold.
JO: Stay with it.
ANDREA: I can't.
JO: You can. You can do it Andy. You can . . . Listen, I'm moving in tomorrow, come and live with me.
From walkway we see KEVIN *picking his wife,* TRISHA, *up and then drive off.*

Streetlife

JO: (*Waves.*) Hi Kev.
JO: What's he supposed to do, leave her? He's responsible for her, that's why I like him. He is wounded see, I ought to let it go. But that's negative, see. If I thought they still had a chance . . Anyway, she's not having him.
ANDREA: He can move in.
JO: Well the courts would take it all, he said, if he moved in. The wife would have it. Hi Mark.
LILY *is dropped off with her father.*

Scene 28: INT. COLLEGE.
The LECTURER *is making a point. She walks around the room.*
LECTURER: People put on a facade . . . people resist their condition like an illiterate pretends he can read, or an alcoholic that he's not drunk . . . Why? Because the illiterate and the alcoholic is full of potential. (*She stops by* JO'S *desk.*) Remember when you were in school? You'd mix the colours yellow and blue – green . . . remember how you felt, Jo?
JO: High as a kite.
LECTURER: Keep doing the work, something will happen.
Scene 29: EXT. DAD'S HOUSE.
Then JO *rushes home – as she nears her dad's home she sees a woman with a suitcase knocking at the door.* JO *looks curiously at the woman. They exchange friendly territorial looks.*
JO: Hallo.
MARY: Hallo. Does Terry Williams live here?
JO: Yes.
MARY: I got the right house then.
JO: (*Shouting through the door.*) What's your name?
MARY: Mary.

JO: (*Shouting again.*) Dad, Mary's here.
DAD (V/O): Mary who? . . .
MARY: Watkins. (MARY *mimics waltzing.*)
JO: (*Through the door.*) Mary Watkins.
   (*To* MARY.) Your dancing partner.
MARY: Down the Legion.
JO: (*Through the door.*) Down the Legion.
(MARY *mimics sexual activity.*)
MARY *nods.* TERRY *appears.*
TERRY: Oh, hallo Mary, come in . . . How's your mother?
   I'll be back in a minute.
JO: Where're you going?
TERRY: Down the shops. What d'you wanna know for?
JO: Get me some chips? I did your washing.
TERRY: That'll take bloody ages.
JO: Oh go on . . .
TERRY *leaves.*
JO: He's like that. (JO *laughs.*)
MARY: It's not funny.
JO *goes around the house making a list, noting the fridge and washing machine.*
MARY: What you doing?
JO: The pub's open.
MARY *leaves.*
JO *goes through house to back lane and whistles the all-clear to van driver.*

Scene 30: EXT. STREET.
The removal van reverses up the lane. LYNWEN *and removal men get out.*

JO: Hiya Mam.
JO: No, that's his. This is mine. Everything with a cross on it, I said. Thanks.
LYNWEN: I'll keep an eye out for your father.

LYNWEN *goes as 'look out' from top of lane.*
Removal men and JO *load the van up.*
JO: No, that's his, everything with a cross on I said.

Scene 31:   JO'S DAD'S HOUSE.   EXT.
JO *comes out. The* REMOVAL MAN *shuts the doors of his van.* JO *waves to* LYNWEN, *who's at the bottom of the street as a lookout. She sees her ex-husband coming.* LYNWEN *runs up the street.*
LYNWEN: He's halfway up the hill. He's coming.
JO: My college books!
REMOVAL MAN: Get in!
JO *rushes back to the house for her briefcase, on the back door we see a note 'Dear Dad, got a place in Legoland. Sorry'*
JO *gets into back of van and it drives off.*
TERRY *walks up hill to his house, followed by* MARY.

Scene 32:   STREET EXT.
JO'S DAD *walks into the house. Across the street curtains twitch. Heads come out of front doors.* JO'S DAD *bellows. He comes out into the street. There's no one in sight. He goes to a house across the street,* JANICE *is watching him.*
TERRY: Janice, what's happening. She's taken the bloody lot!
ANNIE: I don't know, I been out the back. Come on in. I'll make you a cuppa.
TERRY: What, she's taken the kettle as well ?

JANICE: I don't know.
As he passes her, he touches her body. There is something sexual in all TERRY'S *body language.* MARY *notices.*

Scene 33:   ESTATE HOUSE.
Time has passed. KEVIN *has painted half the front room white. He's in a mood. Silent.* JO *watches the camera. Reveals* MARK *painting also.* JO *half smiles.*
KEVIN *follows* JO *outside.*
LILY *sulkingly paints.*
JO: I'm off. Won't be long.
KEVIN *follows* JO.
KEVIN: What you ask him for?
   Why'd you do that?
JO: Why shouldn't I get help? He's a drip, Kevin. You wouldn't understand.
KEVIN: I don't want you to see him.
JO: It's not like that. You're jealous.
KEVIN: 'Course I'm jealous. You're still in a relationship with Lily's dad.
JO: I'm always gonna be in a relationship with Lily's dad. Look, I need help. I want college to work. You're just insecure you are and whether you like it or not, Lily's got a father and it isn't you.

Streetlife

Streetlife

Scene 34: INT. FPA CLINIC.
DOCTOR: Look Jo, you're 18 weeks . . . I can't make the decision for you . . .
JO: I want to have the baby, but I don't want to lose Kevin.

Scene 35: EXT. ESTATE NEAR JO'S HOUSE.
JO *sits on a wall, thinking. She sees women with babies. A street cleaner drives past, she sees a handicapped man struggling on his bike and a man* (EDDIE.) *walking with a cross.*

Scene 36: INT. JO'S NEW HOUSE.
KEVIN *is alone. The place is a lot prettier.* KEVIN *has been putting up shelves.*
JO *enters, she looks round room and is thrilled.*
KEVIN: I got you this, and this.
KEVIN *produces a print for the wall and a bottle of Malibu.*
KEVIN: You're gonna need some furniture, and a sofa. One day we could move to West Wales, Ireland . . .
KEVIN : (*Drinks*) I've outgrown her and she's boring , not like you. We can travel. I got friends in Dublin, America, it's an exciting life see. There's another world out there from this village – confidence. That's what you give me Jo.
JO *hangs onto* KEVIN'S *every word.*
We've gotta live our dreams .
JO *and* KEVIN *are cuddled up now. Two bugs in a rug.*
Then my mother left, I haven't seen her since . . . you move on.

I used to be a terrible liar. I can't do it anymore see
KEV *is nice to her. Tenderness. Pina Coladas. Gentle kissing. Touching each other. Not making love, just touching. Music.*

KEVIN: You know you're not a sexual thing see, with me (*Pause.*) . . . I know I'm married.
JO: Sssh (*Kisses him.*) It's the same for me. We're just a pair of kids you and me. We're in love, that's not going away. Oh Kev. My baby . . .

JO *sits astride* KEVIN. JO *stares into* KEVIN'S *eyes.*

JO: Ooh look at these.
JO: Hold still. (*She squeezes.*) Don't she ever get these blackheads for you?

KEVIN *feels the weight of* JO'S *stomach on him.*

They're in deep. There see.
KEVIN: (KEV *feels* JO'S *stomach.*)
What's this?

JO *kisses him, smiles sweetly, turns away.*

JO: (*Pause.*) I'm pregnant Kev.
KEVIN: Great. It's mine is it?
JO: Kevin Williams!
KEVIN: Joke. (*He hugs her. He smiles to himself unhappily.*) Boy or girl?
JO: I don't know. What do you think . . . You want it?
KEVIN: It's up to you isn't it . . . if you want it . . . I want it . . . (KEVIN *looks at his watch.*)
JO: I want the baby Kev, and I want you.
KEVIN: (*Smiles.*) OK by me. I gotta go now. Last night she rang the Samaritans. We'll talk, OK.

KEVIN *tries to leave.*

JO: When can I see you?
KEVIN: Thursday. I'll come down Thursday.

JO KISSES KEVIN.

JO: My baby...

KEVIN: I'm off. And get a decent carpet will you. I got bits all
over my jacket.
He gets to the door and looks at the ceiling.
What you need here Jo is a big chandelier.
KEVIN *leaves.* JO *is happy but confused.*
Montage Scene:
Bright daylight. JO'S *empty flat, close up.* JO *looks around.*

Scene 37: IRONING ROOM.
Forty black bags are piled into the back of a van. The driver is
DONALD, *an unexciting young man in his late twenties.* DONALD
wears 'right on' clothes and PC badges. JO *is stacking the bags,
neatly clipping them to envelopes containing names and change.
In the background sweating over ironing boards are* LYNWEN,
Jo's mother, ANDREA *her younger sister,* JANICE *and a
contemporary of* LYNWEN, GAIL, *a friend of* JO'S *and a few others.*
JO *is always in a hurry. The music playing is Neil Young
'Someone is Looking at Me', which* JO *accompanies. As* JO
works she concentrates on the idle DONALD, *who is arguing with*
LYNWEN.
DONALD: (TO LYNWEN.) Look Lynwen, I got to take time off I've
got my wife keeping on to me about being there when she has
the baby and there's this bloke I'm seeing . . .
JO: Stop whinging Donald.
LYNWEN: What it is, Donald wants the day off when his wife has
the baby.
JO: Well he can't can he – he's working.
LYNWEN: What Donald means is that a man's gotta be there for
his wife when she's having the baby, right Donald?
DONALD: Yeah.

Streetlife

JO: Well let me tell you something Donald, she don't want you there, telling her to breathe in, breathe out. A man's place is at work so when she's having it you should be here doing what you usually do, chopsing. What you gonna call the baby? Giro?

DONALD: You shut your gob and look at your own life before judging other people.

LYNWEN: You leave her alone and get the bags in the van.

The final bags are placed in the van and DONALD *gets in and drives off.*

SHARON: Jo's in a good mood, getting her ten inches is she?

LYNWEN: I don't think he's that big.

JUNE: Oh, he is. Well, that's what I heard.

JUNE – *embarrassed – looks into the bag.*

Where's that yellow shirt? I can't see for looking.

GAIL (*Laughs.*)

Oooh.

GAIL *catches* JO'S *eye.*

(*To* JO.) What's the matter?

Scene 38: INT. TOILETS, IRONING ROOM.

JO *walks in.* GAIL *follows.*

JO: I need the money Gail.

GAIL: You know what you got to do.

JO: (*whispers.*) I'm pregnant.

GAIL: They won't notice . . .

JO: I will.

GAIL: Don't look at me like that. You're hardly an innocent.

JO *notices* GAIL *is sniffing up some cocaine.*

That was nice.

Scene 39:   GAIL'S HOUSE   INT.

LILY *is playing in* GAIL'S *toilet.* JO, ANNIE & GAIL *drink.* GAIL *is dressed in exotic underwear.*

GAIL: We start in the bathroom – wash their little cocks nice and clean – don't want to catch anything dirty – and then we take them into the bedroom. My oral is brilliant.

You OK?

JO: Fine.

GAIL: Well, you look like shit.

You've got to invest in yourself.

My first week was awful. I let those cowing men take the piss out of me. One man said 'How big are your nipples?' Well I thought he had the right to ask, so I measured them. Lesson number one. Genuine people don't care what you look like.

The phone rings. The girls enter the kitchen – ACKER *is in there.*

Acker, out, this is my space.

ACKER *leaves and* GAIL *picks up the phone*

GAIL: (*Phone.*) Hi Peter darling, how are you?

Hi baby, tell me what you're doing.

(*To girls.*) Trick is to get them off the phone as quick as you can. This one puts the fear of God in me. He wants a free shag. (*phone.*) Come on Peter. Do it on the phone or not at all. You love me when I'm firm – I'll spank you Peter.

Oh, oh, oh, oh . . .

(*To girls.*) Light me a fag.

(*Phone.*) Bye bye Peter, you will phone me again?

(*To girls.*) Wanker.

JO: So, d'you think I should go and see Kev's wife?

GAIL'S *face says this is a bad idea.*

GAIL: No way. Here. (*She gives* JO *a hundred quid.*) Buy the

bloody chandelier. The carpet you'll have to work off though.
JO *notices the Rolex. She takes the money.*
GAIL *goes into toilet, to see* LILY *making a mess.*
GAIL: Lily, what you doing?!

Montage scene:
JO *on the phone, taking sexy phone calls.*
Furniture delivered and carpet laid.
A home at last.

Scene 40: JO'S BEDROOM. INT.
JO *is spraying* EDDIE'S *penis with a new product intended to produce a permanent erection. Effect.* JO *takes in the label.*
JO: You'll have to stroke it, Ed.
ED: Will it work?
JO: Yes.
ED: Marvellous.
JO: Is that it?
ED: Yeah . . .
LILY *comes in and catches* JO *on the bed with* ED. JO *looks up and sees her. On the table a pile of five pound notes next to the phone is a clock.*
JO: Lily, get out!
   I can't do this. I'm sorry Ed, here.
   Lily, your mam's here.
JO *picks up the money, gives half of it back to* EDDIE.

Scene 41: INT/EXT CHINESE TAKEAWAY.
JO *waits for chips. A racist* MAN *with dog is at counter.*
MAN: Hey slant eyes, where's my fucking chips?

Streetlife

CHINESE MAN *rambles on in Chinese*
JO *collects her chips and leaves.*

Scene 42: EXT. STREET.
JO *walks up from Castle grounds eating her chips.*

Scene 43: EXT. STREET.
JO *sits on wall eating chips, a police car pulls alongside* JO.
PC KEITH JENKINS: Anything wrong love?
JO: No.

Scene 44: EXT. STREETS.
JO *is walking home. She looks up and sees* KEVIN *with* SHARON.
KEVIN *starts to kiss* SHARON *but* SHARON *sees* JO *first and pushes* KEVIN *away. The couple separate.*
JO *chases* SHARON. SHARON *reaches home and slams the door.*
JO: Kev! I'll 'ave you, Sharon.
JO *turns on* KEVIN *but* KEVIN *has gone up the hill.* JO *goes after him.*

Scene 45: INT. SHARON'S HOUSE.
SHARON *is safe indoors.*
SHARON'S DAD: What's up, Sharon?
SHARON: Nothing, Dad. Kids alright?
SHARON'S DAD: Asleep upstairs.

Scene 46: EXT. STREET.
KEVIN *marches up the street, followed by* JO.
KEVIN: Nothing happened.
JO: You had your arm around her.

Streetlife

KEVIN: No I never.

JO: I saw you.

KEVIN: You're so clever now you're in college, you can see in the dark!

JO: If you think I'm competing with Sharon Jones . . .

KEVIN: I only went for a curry and she came with me. We met by accident. I'm telling you the truth.

JO: You said you were in Bristol.

KEVIN: I was looking for a job . . . (KEVIN *stops. Anxious.*)
I told you to stop following me.

JO: Afraid I'll see the little house on the prairie?
Afraid I'll see your wife as well . . . maybe I should walk in there and show her this?
I thought you wanted this baby . . .

KEVIN: Come here. Come here. It's not what you think.

He holds the struggling JO.

Ssh. I want the baby. I was with the boys. I bumped into Sharon outside the Railway. All we did was talk.
Nothing happened, right.

He pulls JO *to him, roughly making love.* KEVIN *ejaculates quickly. Trousers on.* JO *is numb.*

JO: Kevin . . . come home with me.

KEVIN: I can't. No I can't Jo. Not tonight.

KEVIN *goes off.* JO *moves off disconsolate.*

Scene 47: INT. IRONING ROOM. MORNING.

JO *and* SHARON *are having a quiet argument. The girls look on amused.*

GAIL: Oprah says, if emotional or sexual problems are distressing, you seek advice.

SHARON: Honest, Jo, you got hold of the wrong end of the stick.
SHARON *keeps on ironing.*
   I'm not apologising for something that never happened.
JO *moves off.*
LYNWEN: What happened?
JO (*To* LYNWEN.): We had a little row, that's all, he'll be back. (*Excuses.*)   That's his thing . . .
LYNWEN: Sulking.
GAIL: Oprah says sulking is a cry for help.
SHARON: He's worried about his wife see . . .   He's gotta stay with her or she'll kill herself.
LYNWEN: She won't. Why blame her, it's not her fault? You always blame somebody else.
ANNIE: She's a bitch. She's been through every man in the corporation. Dirtiest person I ever saw. Even the dogs in the street have shagged her.
JANICE: Look, shut up. If you gotta work at it, it's not working. You wanna change him ? Why don't you find the person you wanna change him into.
ANDREA: Does he want the kid?
JO: Course he does, yeah . . .
LYNWEN: Yeah, men believe everything when they're saying it, an hour later they've forgotten.
LYNWEN *shakes her head.* JANICE *joins her in a conspiratorial duo.*
JANICE (*Interrupts.*): If you ask me, he's trying to keep both balls in the air without dropping one of them. So what does a man do when he has two balls in the air ?– He cops out of both – goes somewhere else. Running away, – what men do best.
GAIL (*About* SHARON.): There's nothing worse though, when you

see someone you love going out with someone bloody drippy, you wonder then what they thought of you.

SHARON: (*Ignores* GAIL.) There's not many fellas like him though, doesn't mind working, paying for the mortgage and everything. I suppose he's tied down, thinking about money.

JO *gets angry.*

JO: What do you mean, tied down? He's getting a divorce.

All the while the music is loud, soulful, sexy.

JO (SHARON.): What's she like then?

SHARON: She's got long dark hair. She's a clerk, I think.
I bet she knows about you.

JO: Let me tell you. When I met Kevin down the Legion – he was so relaxed. Cool. Really sweet. So I just picked him up. I told him about Lily, they don't usually want to know. A single mum – a quick shag. And then I said – 'D'you know what I want Kev? What I really want.– What would make me happy? I want a house in the country, chickens and green wellies.' And he smiled and said 'O.K. you're on.' Then I took him home and we fell in love.

Montage scene:

Opens poster.

JO *watching* TV (*Suicide story*).

Notes in calendar.

JO *on phone to* KEVIN.

Scene 48: INT. JO'S HOUSE.

JO *has cooked* KEVIN *a meal. A big chandelier hangs from the ceiling.*

LYNWEN: Stop it, you'll hurt the baby.

JO: I'm fat without it Mam.

Streetlife

LYNWEN: You're not fat. I was the same with you, I bet it's a girl.
JO: I've messed up, haven't I? I'll terminate it, there's still time. I don't want the kid if he's gonna mess about.
LYNWEN: Jo, you gotta look at his relationship with his own son. Look, you stay with Kevin, you lose college, you lose time with Lily. You've got a baby coming and you've got a man baby. Eh, listen Jo, you got 3 frogs on a wall, one decides to jump, how many are left?
JO: 2?
LYNWEN: No, 3 Jo. The frog made the decision, but did bugger all about it.

Phone rings – JO *rushes to answer it.*

JO: See.

JO *is on the phone to* KEVIN.

JO: Where are you . . . in the pub . . . I haven't heard a word from you in 3 weeks, haven't seen you for a couple of months. . . . Yeah, I know you're looking for a job . . . I did some college work . . . All those plants you bought have blossomed.
I bought the chandelier . . . I know . . . You can do anything you put your mind to . . . do you ever feel like that . . . I'm doing well in college . . . You're wonderful Kev, best thing I did was go with you . . . I'm lucky see, I've got you and Lily and I sorted it with Sharon . . . yeah, I know you gotta live your dreams . . . Nothing wrong is there . . .

Phone down.

LYNWEN *looks on sadly.*

JO: He's not coming round.

JO *puts meal in bin.*

Montage scene:
JO *looking at bills.*
JO *cutting out sayings.*
JO *in mirror – touches belly.*
JO *rushes upstairs –* LILY *is alone in bath.*
JO *listens to radio.*

Scene 49: INT. DRUG HOUSE.
The junkies hang about in a haze of uselessness.
ANDREA *injects. They hear a noise – it's the women searching downstairs.*
ACKER: What's that?
MARZI: Vigilantes.
LYNWEN, JANICE & ABBY *search downstairs and make their way upstairs into room.*
JANICE: Acker! Here they are, where's my Darren?
ABBY: Janice, here he is.
LYNWEN: (*To* ANDREA.) Come on, you're coming home Andrea, look at the state on you.

JANICE *drags her son out.*
LYNWEN *drags* ANDREA *out,* ANDREA *looks out through window and notices arrival of police.*
ANDREA: Shit, it's the police!
The junkies flee the room, ANDREA *goes back for* MARZI.

ANDREA: Marzi, come on!
Everyone rushes downstairs.

LYNWEN *is forced against the bannister and falls to the floor,*

badly hurt, as people rush past her. Two men come upstairs to her.
LYNWEN: Ow, my chest, I can't breathe . . .

Scene 50:   HOSPITAL X-RAY DEPARTMENT. INT.
LYNWEN *is in a wheelchair, having had x-rays taken. The doctor goes out to see* JO *and* ANDREA, *in the waiting room..*
DOCTOR: *(To* LYNWEN.*)* I won't be a minute. *(To* JO/ANDREA.*)* Well, no broken bones . . . quite a lot of bruising. I'd like to keep her in for a few days.
JO: Thank you. Can we see her?
LYNWEN *is wheeled out to waiting room.*
JO: You OK Mam?
LYNWEN: It hurts Jo. Why don't you listen, Andrea?
   Take me home Jo
JANICE *arrives.*
JO: *(To* JANICE.*)* Where's Lily?
JANICE: I left her with your father..
JO *rushes out.*

Scene 51:   JO'S DAD'S HOUSE. INT.
JO *goes into the house. It's quiet.* JO *goes into the bedroom, expecting to find her 4-year old baby daughter asleep in the bed, but* LILY *isn't there.* JO *looks into her father's bedroom. The* TV *is on. The baby,* LILY, *is in bed with her grandfather,* TERRY.
TERRY: There you are.
JO: Dad, give her to me. Lily, come to your Mam.
TERRY: She's a spoil sport.
JO: I never want to see Lily in bed with you, ever again.
TERRY: What you getting at girl? Spit it out.
JO: You know what I'm getting at.

Streetlife

TERRY: We always used to watch TV in bed, me, you, Andrea, your Mum. When you were kids, it was a treat, it was cold. . . .

JO: Dad, give her to me . . .

TERRY *hands over* LILY. JO *takes* LILY *down the stairs.*

JO: Did Grandad touch you?

I'll kill him. I'll bloody kill him. Come downstairs with me, sleep on the settee and we'll go home.

JO *holds* LILY *tight.* LILY *is very tired and is soon asleep.* TERRY *comes in and takes a can of beer off table.* JO *ignores him.*

TERRY: Self-righteous little bitch. You never saw me looking when you were feeding her right here under my eyes.

JO *goes to leave but* TERRY *will not let her.*

TERRY: Look at these. (*Shows her his hands.*)

Worked hard, for what? Your mother leaves me, your sister's a junkie and you are bringing a bastard into the house . . . (*pause,*) . I'm sorry . . . but don't you give me any of that abuse shit. I never laid a hand on you. Come on ,dance with me.

TERRY *pulls* JO *close to him. He is very strong.* JO *goes along with it.*

JO: You'll upset Lily.

TERRY: Come on then.

JO: Stop it, Dad. I'm feeling giddy.

TERRY: Giddy. Not with me you're not.

JO: Stop it. Stop it.

He presses close to her.

TERRY: What's the matter, can't you see I'm dancing?

That's all I'm doing, like the old days.

JO: I don't like it.

He is now struggling to hold her.
His stomach is close to JO'S. *The image is repulsive.*
MARY *enters and stares.* TERRY *leaves.*

Scene 52: INT. JO'S HOUSE.
JO *gets into bed with* ANDREA. *They cuddle up.*
ANDREA: You OK . . . About the baby?
JO: Of course. Yeah . . . it'll be nice for Lily. Too late now.
(*Laughs. Pause.*)
ANDREA: You miss him?
JO: Yeah . . . I love him . . . it's like a disease . . .
He's on my mind all the time and when he's not there . . . I'm nobody. Ssh. Wait.
A noise. The door downstairs opens. JO *goes to investigate.*
JO: What are you doing here?
KEVIN: What d'you think I'm bloody doing here?
JO: This isn't your bloody home. Get out.
KEVIN *goes into the kitchen.*
JO: I said, get out! I haven't seen you for 2 months. Piss off.
JO: You lied to me, you said you met Sharon by accident.
KEVIN: I did.
JO: You said you were getting a divorce.
KEVIN: I will, I am. She's being difficult.
JO: She's a cow . . . your wife . . . and Sharon's a bitch.
KEVIN: (*Interrupts.*) She wanted a shoulder to cry on – I was drunk. I been away Jo . . . looking for work.
JO: But you slept with her.
KEVIN: No .. not proper .. I was pissed. You know what I'm like when I'm pissed. And I couldn't sleep in the van, Jo!
JO: I'll think about it. Now go.

KEVIN: No.
JO: I didn't see what a good deal I had on my own.
KEVIN: Jo . . .
JO: You're not in this relationship. You've never been in. You led me up the garden path . . .
KEVIN: It's her . . . I can't.
JO: You don't love me ,do you? The emotions you just talk about.
KEVIN: You're possessive Jo.
JO: You call me possessive? Yes I do need you. (*She holds her stomach.*)
    I need, I need. I'm not apologising for it. I want this kid.
KEVIN: So do I. So maybe we should get out of this village and see . . .
JO: The world? It's a dream. You're a dreamer Kev. You haven't been anywhere. Love you. I hate you. You're all lies.
Now I am tired, I'm going back to bed. Go back to your wife . . . (*Tenderly.*) . . . please . . .
KEVIN *teases* JO *in a Mexican stand off. She cannot resist him. She sinks to the ground.*
KEVIN: Jo.
JO *crawls across the room.* KEVIN *is irresistible. She smiles and looks up at the bulge in his trousers. He looks down at her triumphant.*
KEVIN: You're a nasty little cow when you're angry.

Scene 53: INT. ANDREA'S BEDROOM.
ANDREA *lies awake listening.*

Scene 54: INT. JO'S BEDROOM (NEXT DAY).
JO *stares at the chocolates* KEVIN *has left on the bed with an affectionate note.*

Scene 55: EXT./INT. SHARON'S HOUSE.
Clutching the chocolates, JO *storms into the street and marches up to* SHARON JONES'S *house.*
JO: What's going on between you and Kev?
SHARON: Nothing. I'm only going out with him.
JO: Only going out with him. Right then, you can keep these bloody chocolates and tell 'im to stop coming down my house and knocking me up bloody crying in the middle of the night any more. . . . oh, and by the way, he told me to tell you, you were a lousy shag – just a bed for the night.
SHARON: They're not worth it are they.
The two of them go inside and sit down.
 I just want a nice house, and I want children, and he doesn't. He doesn't like kids. He hates them.
 He's got kids all over the bloody place and he hates them.
 I'm on about Benny now – not your Kev – (*Pause.*) Cup of tea?
 I don't suppose you like being made a fool of any more than me. Cup of tea? The sex wasn't very good and he did ask me to set up home with him and everything.
JO: You're so stupid, Sharon, but, be fair. You're any bugger's. Poor man's bloody whore. I'm not trying to be bitchy or anything.
SHARON: Come on Jo, get it out.
JO: I mean you were the laughing stock.
SHARON: I know, I always got steamed up.
JO: I mean, I saw them carrying you out the pub stripped off. You used to wear the same bloody dress, arse hanging out, scruffy as hell .
SHARON: Look – it's not Kevin I want. It's Benny – you haven't

seen him have you? Nor me.
So – you keeping it?
JO *relaxes. Smiles.*
JO: Yeah.
They tuck into the chocolates.
SHARON: Couple of bloody mugs, aren't we?

Scene 56: INT. HOSPITAL
LYNWEN *is sleeping.* JO *is watching her mother and looking at the calendar, she writes* '30' *for 30 weeks on her hand.*
LYNWEN *wakes up.* JO *puts two cigarettes under* LYNWEN'S *pillow.*
JO: Hiya Mam.
LYNWEN: Hiya Jo. You phoned John from the Insurance about my money?
JO: (*Lies.*) Yeah.
LYNWEN *looks desperate. She starts to cough.* JO *looks on desperate.*
LYNWEN: You got to Jo. It's important, I need the money.
The pressure begins to tell on JO. LYNWEN *calms down.*
LYNWEN *reaches out to* JO'S *stomach.*
LYNWEN: How big's my little baby?
JO: (*Lies.*) Eighteen weeks (*Pause.*) I'm back with Kev.
LYNWEN: What are we going to do with you?

Scene 57: STREETS. EXT.
JO *and* LILY *walk down a hill to* JO'S *house, chatting with a woman.* JO *is calm. She's happier. They pass a group of women, standing by a car with the radio on.*
WOMAN: Hey Jo, listen to this –

Streetlife

RADIO REPORT

'The residents in Seaton Street in Pontypridd were left dumfounded after thieves pinched their pavements. The culprits, claiming to be council workers, dug up their antique paving stones worth almost £7,000. Police are following up several positive lines of enquiry but no arrests have been made.'

Scene 58: JO'S HOUSE. EXT.

KEVIN *is loading paving slabs from one van to another, outside* JO'S *house.*

ANDREA *walks up to him.*

ANDREA: Where's Jo?

KEVIN: She's in the house.

JO: (*From window.*) Hi.

ANDREA: I need a fiver Jo . . .

KEVIN: Try the lottery.

ANDREA: Bollocks. Why should I subsidise Jeffrey Archer's trips to the Opera

JO: (*From window.*) Stop arguing. I'll be down now.

KEVIN: Go on a course.

ANDREA: For £30 a week? And the promise of a job that never materialises?

JO *comes down and gives her money.* ANDREA *goes upstairs.*

JO *and* KEVIN *sit on sofa in garden.*

KEVIN: Have the baby.

JO: My ex said that. Have the baby.

KEVIN: You can have an abortion.

JO: No. It's too late for that. I could have the baby adopted. I could give it away. I could fall down and they could operate and maybe the baby would die – it would be better if the baby did die. I don't want the baby fostered. That's for sure.

I don't want to give it away to anybody.

KEVIN *looks up to* ANDREA *in window.*

KEVIN: We're never alone are we, here?

JO: Kev, I'm just trying to improve myself. If Andrea or Mark looks after Lily...

KEVIN: I'm off.

JO: No, Kev. I got rights too. We can talk, you're living with her . . . OK. I'll stop him coming, on condition you come and live with me. Look, if you live with me, it'll be OK.

KEVIN: You're losing your temper.

JO: I'm sorry.

KEVIN: You always apologise. Don't apologise.

JO: I'm not . . .

KEVIN: Yes you are.

JO: I'm not Kev.

KEVIN: You are . (*Laughs.*) (*Holds her, kisses her.*) We can't have a relationship that depends on you having your own way all the time. So back off. There's two people in this relationship.

JO: (*Laughs.*) Yeah, you and your wife. You're like Dracula, you're sucking me dry.

KEVIN *starts to laugh. Plays Dracula. Stops.*

KEVIN: I've got a job in Saudi.

JO: Are you going?

KEVIN: Yeah. We need the money.

They start to kiss tenderly.

The phone rings in flat upstairs.

ANDREA: (*From window.*) Jo, Gail's on the phone – she says it's important.

JO: What's it about?

ANDREA: (*From window.*) I dunno, it's personal.

JO: Can you look after Lily?
ANDREA: No, I can't, I'm off.
KEV: I will.
JO: Kev, I want to have the baby and live happily ever after.
JO *goes off to* GAIL'S.

Scene 59: GAIL'S HOUSE. INT.
The floor of the toilet and hall is covered with paper and water.
GAIL *is ceremoniously holding a nappy..Taken from the lavatory.*
The plumber works on.
GAIL: Will you dispose of that please? I can't have Lily here. Not with clients. You treat me like a chamber maid – just 'cos you've got a baby, You're so selfish. I set this up. You breeze in thank you very much, well I'm paying for this.
JO: That's enough Gail.
GAIL: Quite right. Enough is enough. You owe me £60 for this and the £100 I lent you.
JO: What for?
GAIL HANDS HER A BILL.
GAIL: The chandelier! I've broken it down. Overheads, phones, 'Will you lend me this? Can you lend me that?' That's you all over. Last week you dumped Lily on me. The baby's a ball and chain .
JO: No she's not.
GAIL: The baby is a problem.
JO: No!
JO *walks out.*
GAIL: Get out! You're stifling me. I want my own space. Perhaps we could see each other as friends sometime?
Oprah'd like that.

Scene 60:   STREET. EXT.
JO *is in tears. Tears become a smile.*
JO: Kevin will love this story. . . .
She rushes towards home.

Scene 61:   JO'S HOUSE. INT.
There's no sign of KEVIN. LILY *is alone. There's a letter on the table.*
JO: Kev, Kev, where are you?
    Kev, Kev, I'm back Kev.
JO *reads letter.*
'*Dear Jo , I have to be absolutely honest with you . . .*'

Scene 62:   STREETS. EXT.
JO *is very lonely.*
She asks people in street where KEVIN *lives.*
JO *looks up and sees* KEVIN'S WIFE *walk up the street. She follows.*
JO *watches a young boy walking away from a fight.*
TRISHA (KEVIN'S WIFE.): Kevin, get here!
She boxes his ears.
TRISHA: You fight him or he'll always beat you up.
    Go on, get him, beat him up, kill him . . .
KEVIN JUNIOR *goes off to fight.* JO *watches.*
The two young boys fight each other. JO *feels the blows.*
TRISHA: They gotta learn to survive . . . I know you . . . you're
    that woman our Kevin had. (*She stares.*) . . . I feel sorry for
    you . . . believing him and all that. I'm glad to see the back
    of him. He's a waste of time. That's it, kill him (*to* YOUNG
    KEVIN.)
JO: D'you know when he's coming back . . . from Saudi ?
TRISHA: Is that what he said, Saudi? You won't find no camels

where he is. Up the Smoke with a tart from Treorchy. *The other boy hits him.* JO *now feels the early pains of premature birth.* JO *feels the blows again, again, again. She breathes deeply.*

Scene 63: INTENSIVE CARE WARD. INT.
LYNWEN *is on a life support machine.*
NURSE: It's pneumonia. It was blood on her lungs.
JO *is confused.*
   (*Pause.*) Someone didn't notice it on the X-ray. The rib punctured her lung.
The nurse walks off. JO *goes over to* LYNWEN.
JO *feels the baby move in her stomach. She stares fearfully around then calms herself. At this point* JO'S *inner resolve has collapsed. The grief for her mother and rejection by* KEVIN *is too much.*
NURSE *goes to medicine trolley,* JO *looks. Another nurse is at the medicine trolley.*
JO: (*To* LYNWEN.) He bought flowers. How can a man love you so much and then change his mind? What am I going to do Mam?
The NURSES *leave the ward.*
JO *goes to medicine trolley and takes bottle of pills.*
JO *leaves.*

Scene 64: STREETS. EXT. NIGHT.
JO *comes out of Hospital. There is a police car across the street. She puts pills tightly in her pocket.*

Scene 65: JO'S HOUSE – BEDROOM.
JO *lies on bed, clutching the pills.*

Scene 66: IRONING ROOM. INT.
The black bags pile up again. The room is empty. JO *goes across to* JANICE.
JANICE: Hiya Jo, how is Lynwen?
JO: (*Shakes her head.*) It's not good.
  I'm going away to have the abortion.
  Afterwards, they say I should rest up – can I stay in the caravan?
JANICE: Course you can love.
  (*Hands her keys.*)
  You managing?
JO: (*Smiles.*) Yes. You know me. I'm a Valley girl
JANICE *watches unsure.* JO *walks off.*

Scene 67: JO'S HOUSE – KITCHEN.
JO *fills bag with food & clothes, to go to the caravan.*

Scene 68: INT. JO'S HOUSE – LANDING.
JO *drops* LILY *off with neighbour across landing.*
NEIGHBOUR: Look after yourself.

Scene 69: INT. BUS/EXT COUNTRYSIDE.
JO *travels on bus to caravan site. She gets off bus and starts walking. As she walks, two dogs run towards her and go for her bag. This shakes* JO *up.* JO *sits & realises her waters have broken*

Scene 70: CARAVAN. INT/EXT.
A kettle is boiling, JO *prepares for the birth.* JO *goes into labour and gives birth and cuts the umbilical cord. She wraps baby in*

towel. The baby is placed in a cardboard box. JO *unpacks nappies, bottles & pills etc.* JO *makes up the baby's milk and unsuccessfully tries feeding her the bottle.* JO *suffers deep hormonal distress. She takes out the sleeping pills and puts them on a spoon before giving them to the baby.*
JO *takes pills herself and sleeps, she wakes to the realisation that the baby is dead.*
JO *puts all the 'evidence' in black bags and dumps one under caravan.* JO *packs her bag and cleans herself up.*

Scene 71: EXT: RIVER'S EDGE.
JO *carries the baby around in a black bin bag. She walks to the edge of the fast flowing river. She looks at the river. In her head it is flowing blood.*
The baby looks like it's dead. JO *puts the baby in the water. She lets go of the baby. The current quickly carries it away.*
JO *walks off.*

Scene 72: JO'S HOUSE. INT.
JO *walks into her house.*
ANDREA *comes from bathroom.*
ANDREA: I'm up here. You alright Jo?
ANDREA, JO & LILY *lie on the bed.*
JO *goes into her own bedroom and takes the baby clothes and the nappies and puts them in a drawer in her bedroom.*

Scene 73: BEACH EXT.
PC KEITH JENKINS *and* FISHERMAN *approach the shore.*
The body of the baby is caught up on some rocks on the shore.
FISHERMAN: The tide's brought it in, the rat's have been at it.

PC KEITH JENKINS *kneels down into water.*
PC KEITH JENKINS: It's a baby.

Montage scene:
REPORTER *approaches* PC KEITH JENKINS *on beach, a white tent is erected for the body.*
REPORTER: What's the story then, Keith?
PC KEITH JENKINS *walks away.*

Scene 74: IRONING ROOM INT.
ANDREA *watches the TV with* JO *and* GAIL *and* JANICE. *The tension between* JO *and* GAIL *is noticeable.*
GAIL: I don't understand it.
JO: You wouldn't.
JANICE: I do. Poor thing.
JO *puts* LILY *on her lap.*
T.V. REPORT:
TV REPORTER (V/O)
'DSI Griffiths, who is leading the hunt for the baby's mother, said that there must be somebody who knows her identity. All information will be treated with the strictest confidence.'
JANICE: Well, I find it hard to believe that a young woman could have given birth to the baby with no one else knowing.
GAIL: Yeah. Someone knows alright.
INSERT:
TV REPORTER (V/O)
'The baby is said to be 6 – 8 weeks premature. The police believe the mother may be suffering from internal injuries.
She must be in great pain. Police will today begin enquiries on major housing estates in South Wales, the Valleys and Cardiff to

Streetlife

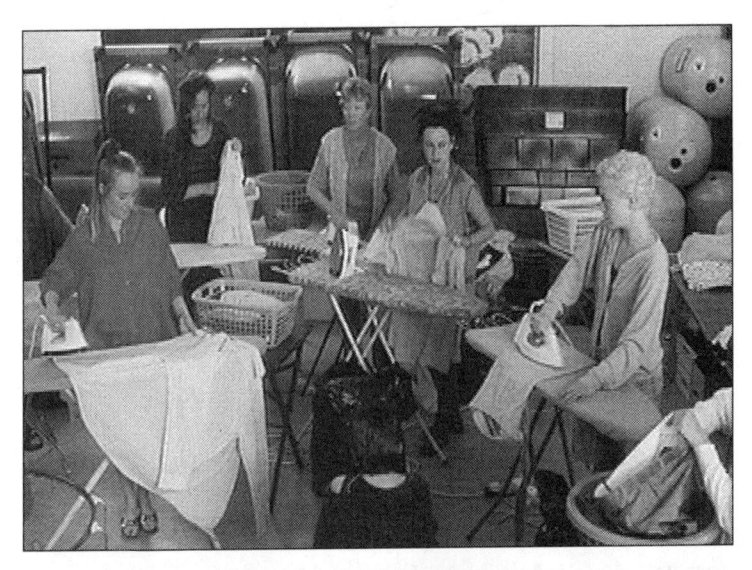

try to trace the mother. Police say they are anxious to trace the mother who seems to have lost an awful lot of blood. The blanket was heavily stained with blood.'
ANDREA: I bet she's hiding in a flat, poor thing.
GAIL: Poor thing, she's a bloody murderer . . . Mad.
JANICE: Mad isn't bad.
The women keep ironing.
JO: (*Interrupts.*) It happens all the time. We had a girl when I was in school – Karen – having a baby in the toilets – that no one knew about.
The TV shows a photofit of a girl – but not like JO.
ANDREA: That's the trouble you got when you find this sort of thing going on. You've got nobody to get angry with.
JANICE: Or feel sorry for.
GAIL: So where's she from? Here?
JANICE: No. Ireland I expect. Off the ferry.
GAIL: Catholic.
JO: Why didn't she have it looked after like I did – just do what she was told.

Scene 75: INT. TOILET.
ANDREA *watches as* JO *climbs the stairs.* JO *goes into the toilet. She takes her blouse off to relieve the pressure on her breasts. Milk comes forth. Below the TV is on.*
TV REPORT:
'The mother will however have an overwhelming urge to talk to someone about what has happened. It is also certain that she needs either emotional or physical help.'
JO *listens intently as she dresses again. Sore . . . and confused . . . tired . . . waiting.*

JO *comes out.* JO *looks out to the men in the street. She sees someone who looks like* KEVIN.
JO: Kev! (*She looks excited.*)
The man looks around. It's not KEVIN.
Inside the ironing room, the phone rings.
ANDREA *rushes out to* JO.
ANDREA: It's Mam!

Scene 76: HOSPITAL. INT. CARE WARD.
ANDREA *and* JO *go in to find that her mother isn't there.*
JO: Where is she?
ANDREA *starts to cry. The* NURSE *leads* JO *down a long corridor across a yard into a small, cheap, sideward.*
JO: You're passing the body back and forwards, why'd you move her?
NURSE: It's cheaper.

Scene 77: A SIDEWARD.
JO *stares at her mother who is still switched on to a machine.*
NURSE: Your mum's not going to get any better. All her body organs are failing. We'll need your permission to switch the machine off.
JO *goes to her mother and kisses her. Looks to* ANDREA.
JO: No. I lost the baby Mam.

Scene 78: EXT. STREETS.
JO *is depressed. She's on her way to the phone box.*
JO *meets up with* GAIL, *who's chatting with a group of women.*
GAIL: Hi.

I'm sorry Jo. Kiss, kiss.

63

JO *kisses* GAIL.
JO: OK.
GAIL: You should sue the hospital for negligence
JO: Yea . . .
GAIL: (*To women as* JO *goes.*) She's out of it, far out.

Scene 79:   PHONE BOX/INCIDENT ROOM.
JO *makes her way to a phone box. She dials the police.*
POLICE OPERATOR: Operations Room.
JO: You won't find her. I'm the mother. She was still born. Leave her go.
POLICE OPERATOR: OK. Hold the line please.
KEITH JENKINS: Hello
JO: I'm the mother of the baby that was found. Leave her alone. You have to. She was still born.
KEITH JENKINS: OK. Take your time, love.
JO: I know you're tracing the call. I'm the mother. Leave her alone. I'm OK. You got to. She was still born. Please.
Phone goes dead.
WPS SIMPSON: What d'you think?
KEITH JENKINS: It's a local girl.

Scene 80:   SHOP'S INT./EXT.
JO *is out shoplifting from a baby clothes boutique. She wants to be caught. She gets a few things and walks out. Nobody stops her.* GAIL *and* JANICE *watch her.*
GAIL: You alright Jo?
JO: Yeah.
JO *and* LILY *walk up street.*

GAIL: Hormones I expect.
JANICE: Yeah
GAIL/JANICE: She's odd, isn't she.

Scene 81:   JO'S HOUSE   INT.
JO goes upstairs quietly, and watches LILY *sleeping, blanking it all out. In the days that have followed there has been no news of the baby. Black bags continue to dominate her life. The place is spotless.*
ANDREA: I'm off it Jo.
JO: I'm skint.
There is news on the TV of the baby.
ANDREA: I'm serious.
They watch the TV together

TV INSERT: MINISTER (*To reporter.*)
'There was never any question of this child having a pauper's funeral.
Everyone has been very good. We've received many calls with offers to help but quite obviously they will not be needed. The mother and the police have my deepest sympathy.'

There is a huge number of people. Also cards, teddy bears, wreaths.
JO: Poor baby.
ANDREA: I feel sorry for the mother.
JO: I don't. I hate her.
MINISTER: Let us remember those times when we have come
    dangerously close to harming our own children.
I believe that when Jesus said 'Suffer little children to come unto

Streetlife

me' he was talking of the mother's grief.
ANDREA: We should go – to that little girl's funeral – you know . . .
JO: Why? It's nothing to do with us. You'll be clucking anyway.
ANDREA: (*Shrugs her shoulders.*) I can't talk to you Jo. You're on another planet.
ANDREA *leaves and comes in to find* JO *still distraught, putting baby boots on* LILY.
ANDREA: Jo? What the hell you doing?
JO: I miss him. I miss him so much.
ANDREA: You haven't been right since the abortion.
ANDREA *lies with* LILY.
JO *exits room with black bags.*

Scene 82: INT. JO'S HOUSE – KITCHEN.
JO *comes from bedroom, goes downstairs and washes her hands in kitchen.*

Scene 83: INT. STAIRWELL.
JO *walks to stairwell and sits on stairs.*
ANDREA: I'll look after you Jo.
JO: You can't look after yourself.
ANDREA: Nobody knows Jo.

Scene 84: EXT. STREETS ON ESTATE.
JO *walks past building being demolished on her way to the ironing room. Police are on the estate with photofits.*
JO *looks worried, she is seen by the women, also on their way to the ironing room.* SHARON *points out article in newspaper.*

Scene 85: INT/EXT IRONING ROOM.

Streetlife

THE *women work. They sense something more is going on with* JO. *Maybe she is the dead baby's mother. No one listens to* GAIL, *who is trying to break the atmosphere.*

GAIL: (T*ells joke.*) Princess Di was thick before she became Princess of Wales so she was sent for elocution lessons, 'Now Diana, you have to learn how to introduce yourself properly '.

JO *enters.*

JO: Dad fucked me, you know. When I was twelve. Told me he didn't want me in the house. I wasn't paying rent. I went mad for a few years. Then I met this bloke in Cardiff. I was terrified of losing him.

I shared a house with 5 men.

Their Christmas present was fucking me.

Then I met Mark . . .

Silence

ANDREA: Jo – we love you – Jo.

JO: I was OK in the day with my first baby – Lily. We'd go for walks in the park. When I'd get home the house was so damp and ugly. It was freezing. I sold everything – the stereo, for nappies, clothes for his dope. He was stealing my soul.

ANDREA: Jo . . .

JO: I was doing my A levels. I wanted to be a primary school teacher.

I had to leave him. He wanted all my attention and I had the baby. He said he felt rejected, didn't change a nappy.

I never went out. He taped stamps over the keyhole. I felt ashamed all the time.

I'm sorry, I'm sorry.

GAIL *looks to* ANDREA *to stop* JO. *Clearly her friends love her, but*

the truth is dawning on some of them.
ANDREA: Jo . . . I can't handle this.
JO *is crying uncontrollably. Her pain is breaking. She runs out,* JANICE *follows her.*
They see a Police car and watch as PC JENKINS *and* WPS SIMPSON *get out.* JO *notices* PC JENKINS *being nice to* LILY. *They have photofit pictures with them. They go into various houses.*
GAIL, JO, JANICE, ANDREA *linger.*
JO: They never give up, do they.
JANICE: Is Lily OK Jo?
JO: Oh yes . . . (*Oblivion.*)
   Dad came for her too, I stopped him.
JO *then starts to cry for her mother.* JANICE *seems to understand.*
JANICE: I know – I'll be your mother.
ANDREA *comes up into group.*
ANDREA: She's got rights too.
JANICE: Just keep your gob shut Andrea.
GAIL: You didn't hurt that baby, did you Jo?
JO: No.
JANICE: Don't you go to that funeral Jo.
JO *goes off.*

Scene 86 – INT. LANDING OF JO'S FLAT.
JO *rushes upstairs past the two police officers. She has a black bag with her. On the landing, she drops it. Things fall out. She picks them up, she rushes into the flat. She hears footsteps on the door. She hears footsteps coming up the stairs.*
PC JENKINS *comes up, finds a baby boot on the landing, comes onto landing, hears a door slamming. All the doors look the same. In his hand is a photofit, not unlike* JO.

Scene 87: INT/EXT. JO'S FLAT.
JO *listens at door. She puts contents of first bag into another bag and packs another.* JO *looks out of window, she sees police coming out of building, going to their car.* JO *turns away from the window.*
She takes the black bags out to the bins, getting rid of the evidence.

Scene 88: CEMETERY EXT.
Silver plaque on white coffin – 'Baby Zoe'. People step forward to put wreaths on the coffin. Zoe – now with the angel from someone who cares. 'Good night and God Bless'. All eyes on KEITH JENKINS *as he carries the coffin.*
Eight uniformed policemen line the steps in a guard of honour as the policeman moves towards the grave.
JO *suddenly appears as if from nowhere, with* ANDREA *pushing* LILY.

MINISTER: We have felt for you who have been so involved in this situation. It has not been easy for you. We place this child before the cross of Christ. Let us pray for the mother, the mother whose pain we cannot understand. Whose reasons for rejecting this child we cannot understand. But a mother who found it necessary in this harsh society to reject her child – let us pray for the mother.

Silence.

Let us pray for the policeman who found her, and for the pain that he has experienced. This child is now at peace with none of the pain and suffering of life today.

Gentle Jesus, Meek & Mild, Look Upon This Little Child.

GAIL *starts to sing 'The Lord's My Shepherd'.* JO *walks to the*

Streetlife

grave, she looks in. She throws dirt on the grave. KEITH JENKINS *catches her eye. He has been crying. She smiles sympathetically. She touches his hand and holds it.* JO *disappears.*

Scene 89: EXT. EMPTY COLLIERY.
JO *walks along the lonely empty colliery track, looking down on the valley below. She hears a sound, looks around – it's* KEITH. *She tries running away from him. He hands her the baby's bootee.*
JO: You found the baby?
KEITH *nods his head.*
   Who called her Zoe?
KEITH: I did, after my mother.
   I held her in my arms.
JO: (*sobbing quietly.*) I'm sorry, I'm sorry, I'm sorry.
KEITH: It's OK Jo, it's going to be OK.
   Don't be frightened.
JO: I hurt my head . . . The day Zoe was born they asked me to switch her off.
   My mother is in hospital.
   It wasn't an accident, it was somebody's fault.
   And Kevin Price is her dad. All I ever wanted was that he'd love me.
   Men are such liars. They say they love you, they say they respect you.
JO *turns away.*
   Please forgive me . . .
   (*To herself.*) I'm the mother.
She turns around, KEITH *isn't there anymore.*
We see KEITH *walking away.*

Streetlife

Scene 89: EXT. EMPTY COLLIERY.
JO *alone against the mountain.*

Streetlife

Cast

jo - Helen McCrory
kevin - Rhys Ifans
gail - Donna Edwards
andrea - Ruth Lloyd
pc jenkins - Jeremi Cockram
mark - Huw Davies
lynwen - Lynwen Hobbs
sharon - Clare Isaac
lily - Gemma Probert
janice - Christine Tuckett
marzi - Richard Harrington
terry - John Pierce Jones
mary - Lynn Hunter
trisha - Nicola Branson
wps simpson - Teresa Hennessy
annie - Clare Erasmus
engineer - Philip Howe
doctor - Julie Higginson
psychiatrist - Wynford Ellis Owen
minister - Brinley Jenkins
fpa doctor - Ray Gravel
photographer - Roger Nott
eddie - Mike Forrest
acker - Russel Gomer
donald - Gary Howe
lecturer - Judith Humphries
creditor - Richard Goodfield
police operator - Helen Veasey
reporter - Philip Rowlands
nurse - Lowri Mae

Streetlife

Streetlife
First screened on BBC2, Screen 2 on the 25th November 1995.

Written and Directed by KARL FRANCIS
Music Composed by JOHN HARDY
Producer RUTH CALEB

First Assistant Director GEOFF SKELDING
Second Assistant Director EUROS LYN
Associate Producer HELEN VALLIS
Script Editors CERI MEYRICK ROBYN SLOVO
Production Designer RAY PRICE
Film Editor ROY SHARMAN
Director of Photography NIGEL WALTERS
Costume Designer JAKKI WINFIELD
Make-up Designer MARINA MONIOS
Location Manager PATRICK SCHWEITZER
Sound RICHARD DYER TIM RICKETTS
PAUL JEFFRIES IAN JOHNSON
Costume Assistant SUZIE LEWIS
Make-up Assistant STEVE WILLIAMS
Buyer GARY FLAY *Stand-by Props* PHIL SHELLARD
Design Op LAURIE GUINEE *P.A* TRACIE SIMPSON
Focus Puller NICK LOWIN *Grips* ALFIE WILLIAMS
Clapper Loader MIKE WARD *Gaffer* ALAN MUHLEY
Electricians STEVE WILLIAMS RICHARD STEVENS
THOMAS MILLIGAN

Streetlife

© Amelia Jones

Streetlife

Notes on a film

Streetlife was conceived originally as a low budget drama for the BBC Screen Two slot. "About 75 minutes" they said. "Real People, no actors, coming at drama from a documentary structure" - not unlike *Ms Rhymney Valley, Mr.Chairman* and *Rough Justice,* three earlier films of mine.

This was in August 1994, and having spent two months in the United States still haunted by the violence of Right Wing Red Neck Radio Christianity, especially their self-righteous views on the single mother, a species they wished to eliminate from the American dream, notwithstanding the Santa Marias of Jesus, nor His deep love and respect of all women, I - through rage and prayer- found myself drawn to this same subject. The photograph in the *Western Mail* of young Constable Davies carrying a white coffin containing the body of a dead, abandoned baby, drew me inevitably into researching infanticide as a film drama subject. Not a happy ending here. Forget Hollywood, I thought. Welsh realism, I thought. Welsh realism. Here we come again.

I soon realised that the tape given me by the Swansea police of a caller claiming to be the mother was another prayer to haunt me and to drive me away from a detective male-centred police investigation into a Greek mythologically inspired media-like story about who this anonymous woman might be. It is precisely because the principles of anonymity- the opposite of hype, particularly when Film Fever rages - had wrapped themselves around this story that I became involved. We are as sick as our secrets, after all, and the skeletons of many a Welsh graveyard awake at opening time to tell a merry tale of hell and low water. And like most valley writers, I have been angry and irritable daily watching the consequences of Tory social policies upon the lives of the young, disappointed unemployed.

So, *Streetlife* began as a 200 page script with voice overs, political analysis, excess- all of which slowly disappeared from the final draft.

I then met the actresses whom I thought could play Jo -Eddie Ladd and Helen McCrory. From the outset Eddie had more problems than I did with the "sexuality" of the role. Helen pursued me for the role with a delightful commitment and, even though I had reservations about her ability to do a 'valleys' accent - she'd left Wales for Africa and England with her parents whilst a young girl - she nevertheless had the greatest of talents and I soon was left without choice or doubt.

The problem we now had was the budget and, despite a real passion for the subject from London Drama - Robyn Slovo the Script Editor had helped me enormously to focus my ideas - there remained some resistance to it. I'd reached a point I'd reached with many other films.

It was my film. I was going to make it any way- with my own money if necessary, and proceed like a poet or a painter. Unlike many film makers, I write and direct. It is very different being a writer/director. I have to kill the writer (me) when I direct (me). It is the writer in whose womb the baby has rested before all the midwives get their hands on it and the fever rises.

Fortunately, Dai Smith, Head of Programmes, English Language, and Ruth Caleb, the producer of *Streetlife* , both wanted a 'child', but it had to be created for an anorexic £310,000, over 20 days, and with full time actors. It was no

Streetlife

longer a cheap documentary. To some it was to become an example of high quality, low cost drama. Indeed, it came as a delight, if not a shock, to many in the BBC when David Hare, the eminent playwright and film-maker, in a BBC Drama Review Board, described it as the best thing in the BBC 1995/96 Drama Season.

Karl Francis 1996

Streetlife

© Amelia Jones

Streetlife: A Film Diary

9th April 1995
Note to Ruth Caleb from Karl Francis

'Jo is a character for the times, who is much bigger than just a woman who has lost her way,' I said to Helen. Helen pursued me because she really wanted to play the part. My fairy godmother must have been watching over me when I found her.

12th April 1995
Note to Dai Smith, Head of Programmes, English Language.

'Helen McCrory's background couldn't be more different from that of the character she plays. The daughter of a diplomat, her mother a Morgan, she was born in Paddington, London, but spent much of her childhood abroad. Can she do the accent? Lived in Wales with grandfather.'

Despite her Welsh roots - Helen's mother was brought up in Cardiff - Wales did not feature greatly in her early years, so mastering the accent was quite a challenge, especially as the nuances and idioms had to be conquered within a week.'

Karl Francis

Streetlife

15th April 1995
Notes
Of her character, Helen says "Jo is ambitious and longs to make something of herself, she has a wonderful imagination and enjoys life hugely. In spite of her background, the love and educational opportunities, she is never motivated by aggression or bitterness or jealousy. She has a lot of fight in her, but it is a fight directed at improving the quality of her life.

Jo also has great strength. Even at the lowest point she doesn't crumble, and she never becomes hard. Perhaps she isn't the wisest thing in the world, and her misplaced trust and faith in people make her vulnerable. She believes that if someone says something, they mean what they say."

Karl Francis

Notes

'The bleak themes underpinning *Streetlife* are frequently defused by humour. The raunchy, raucous humour of Jo and her women friends celebrates the ability of the human spirit to rise above adversity. Writer and director Karl Francis says the idea behind the film was the discovery of a baby's body in Swansea Marina. Rather than damn the mother as a monster, he thought of the larger picture and the events in the woman's life which led to such a desperate action. '

Ruth Caleb to Dai Smith.

Streetlife

'*Streetlife* weaves a tale which could have parallels with that of a mother who disposed of her newly born child. It tells the story without making moralistic judgements.'
Francis to Caleb.

'She is ambitious and longs to make something of herself, she has a wonderful imagination and enjoys life hugely. In spite of her background, the lack of love and educational opportunities, she is never motivated by aggression or bitterness or jealousy. She has a lot of fight in her, but it is a fight directed at improving the quality of her life.

'Filming was completed in 20 days. Lansbury Park estate in Caerphilly provided the austere backdrop for the drama. Like the fictitious estate in *Streetlife,* Lansbury Park suffers from economic deprivation, but Karl Francis has nothing but praise for the people who live there.

It has a reputation for being a very poor estate, but poverty of spirit was no way evident. The generosity of the people was incredible. People can make life very difficult for you when you are filming, but this was not the case here.'
Ruth Caleb.

Helen McCrory on Jo.

'No-one is in the best situation to make an objective character assessment when they have fallen in love. Kevin appeals to Jo because he has a childlike quality, he too longs to be someone and make something of his life, and these attributes are very rare in her world.'

Streetlife

Streetlife